The big wet balloon

LiNiErs

THE
BIG WET
BALLOON

A TOON BOOK BY

LINIERS

TOON BOOKS • NEW YORK

PARENTS MAGAZINE 10 BEST CHILDREN'S BOOKS
EISNER AWARD NOMINEE
ALA GRAPHIC NOVEL READING LIST

For Matilda and Clementina ... my little muses

Editorial Director: FRANÇOISE MOULY

Book Design: FRANÇOISE MOULY & RICARDO LINIERS SIRI

LINIERS'S artwork was done using ink, watercolor, and drops of rain.

A TOON Book™ © 2013 Ricardo Liniers & TOON Books, an imprint of RAW Junior, LLC, 27 Greene Street, New York, NY 10013. No part of this book may be used or reproduced in any manner whatsoever without written permission except in the case of brief quotations embodied in critical articles and reviews. TOON Graphics™, TOON Books®, LITTLE LIT® and TOON Into Reading!™ are trademarks of RAW Junior, LLC. All rights reserved. Library of Congress Cataloging-in-Publication Data: Liniers, 1973- The big wet balloon : a TOON book / by Liniers. pages cm. -- (Easy-to-read comics. Level 2) Summary: "Matilda promises her little sister Clemmie an amazing weekend spent playing outside. But the weather's rainy and Clemmie can't bring her new balloon along. Matilda teaches Clemmie all the delights of a wet Saturday"-- Provided by publisher. ISBN 978-1-935179-32-0 (alk. paper) 1. Graphic novels. [1. Graphic novels. 2. Sisters--Fiction. 3. Rain and rainfall--Fiction. 4. Balloons--Fiction.] I. Title. PZ7.7.L56Bi 2013 741.5'973--dc23 2012047662 All our books are Smyth Sewn (the highest library-quality binding available) and printed with soy-based inks on acid-free, woodfree paper harvested from responsible sources. Printed in China by C&C Offset Printing Co., Ltd. Distributed to the trade by Consortium Book Sales & Distribution, a division of Ingram Content Group; orders (866) 400-5351; ips@ingramcontent.com; www.cbsd.com. A Spanish edition, *El globo grande y mojado*, is also available. ISBN: 978-1-935179-32-0 (hardcover English edition)
ISBN: 978-1-943145-47-8 (softcover English edition)
ISBN: 978-1-935179-39-9 (Spanish softcover edition)
19 20 21 22 23 24   C&C   10 9 8 7 6 5 4
WWW.TOON-BOOKS.COM

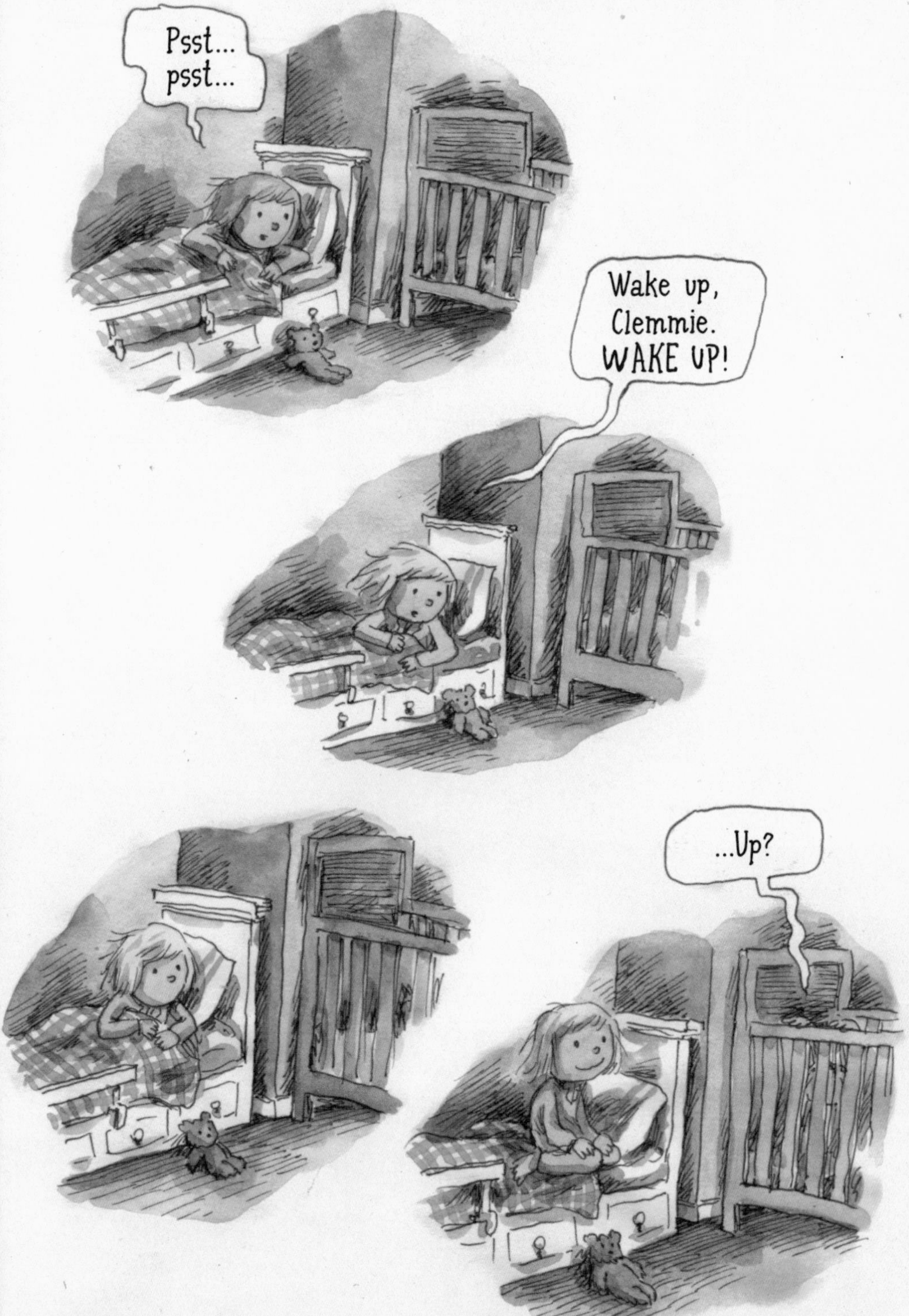
Psst... psst...
Wake up, Clemmie. WAKE UP!
...Up?

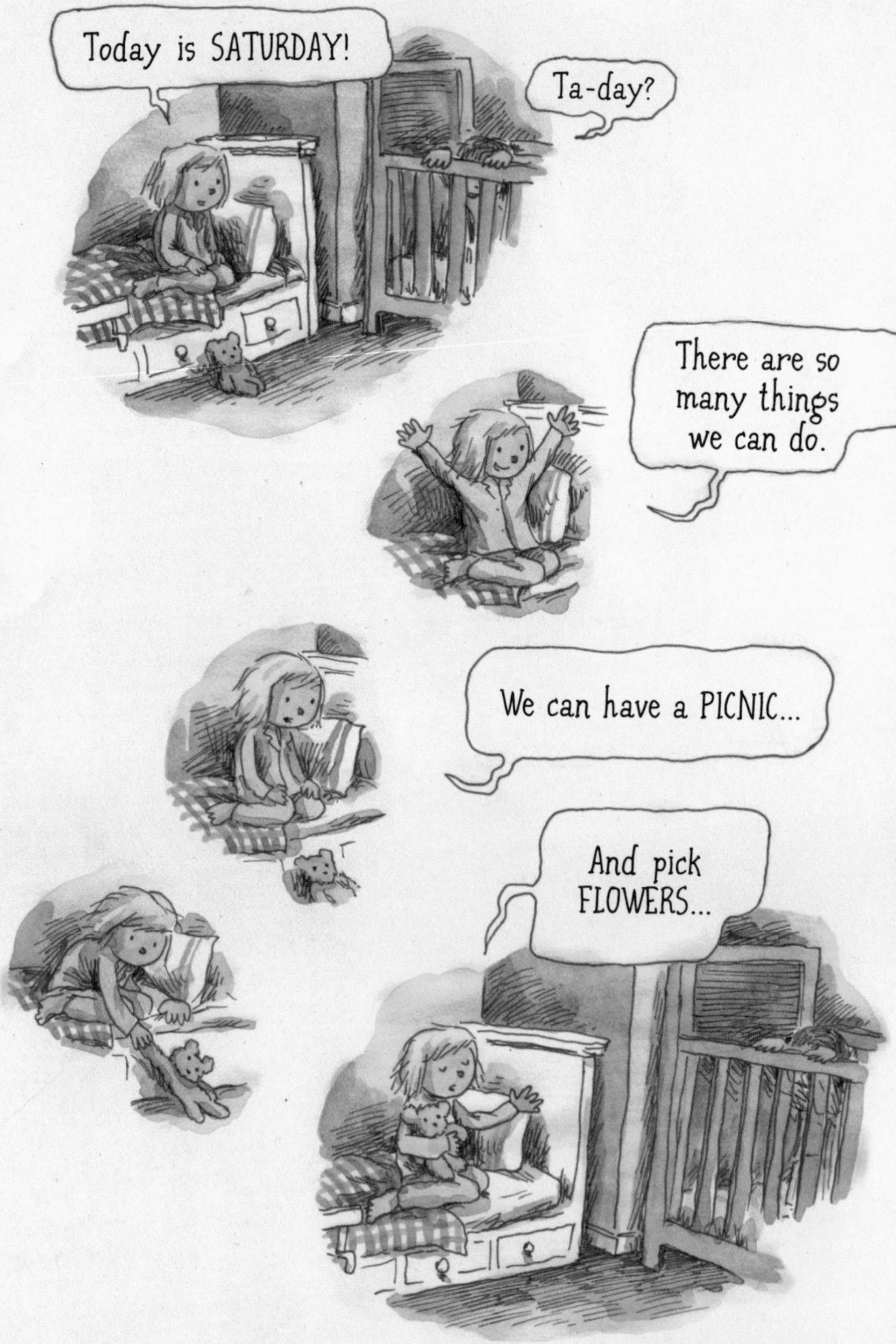
Today is SATURDAY!
Ta-day?
There are so many things we can do.
We can have a PICNIC...
And pick FLOWERS...

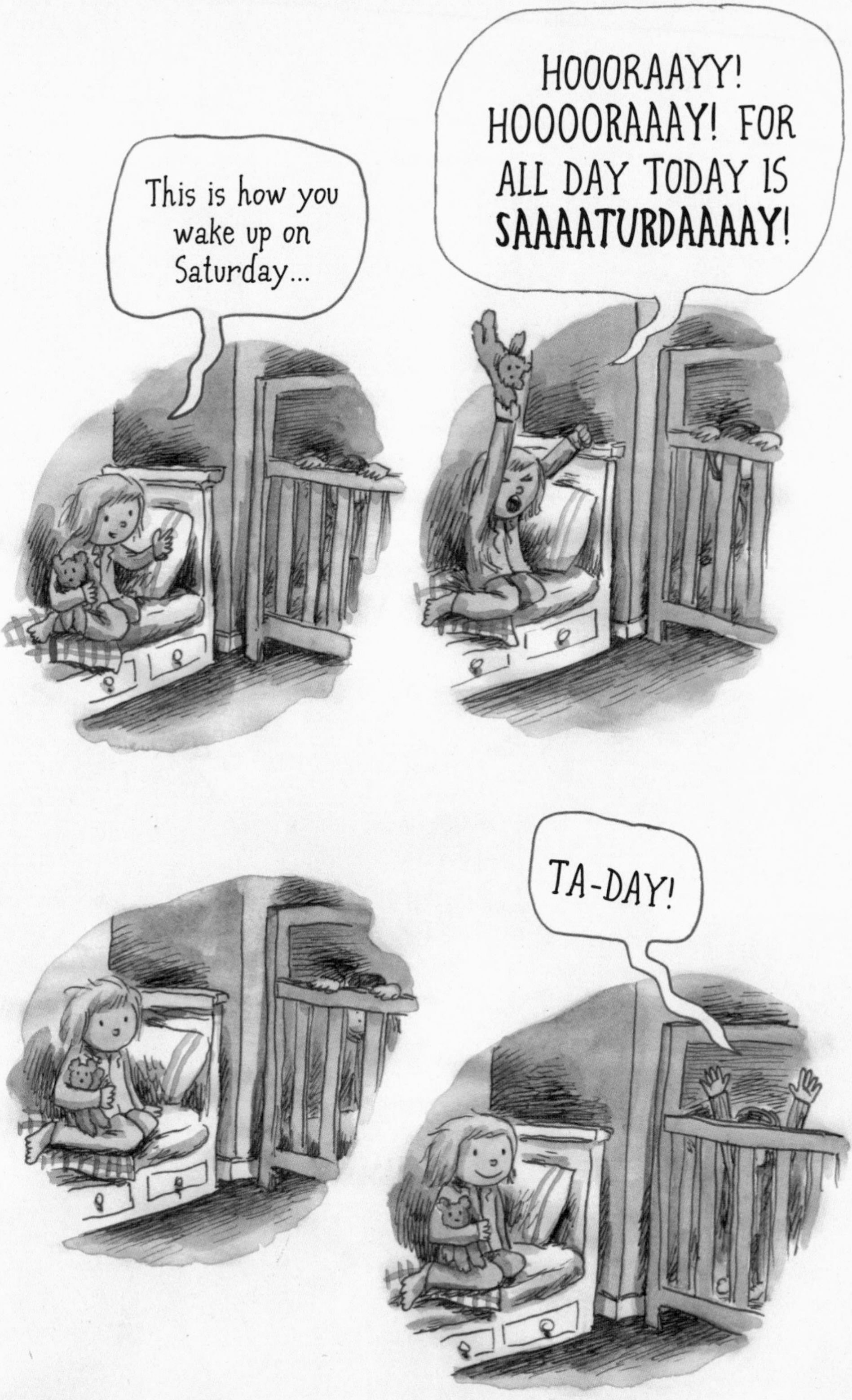
This is how you wake up on Saturday...
HOOORAAYY! HOOOORAAAY! FOR ALL DAY TODAY IS SAAAATURDAAAAY!
TA-DAY!

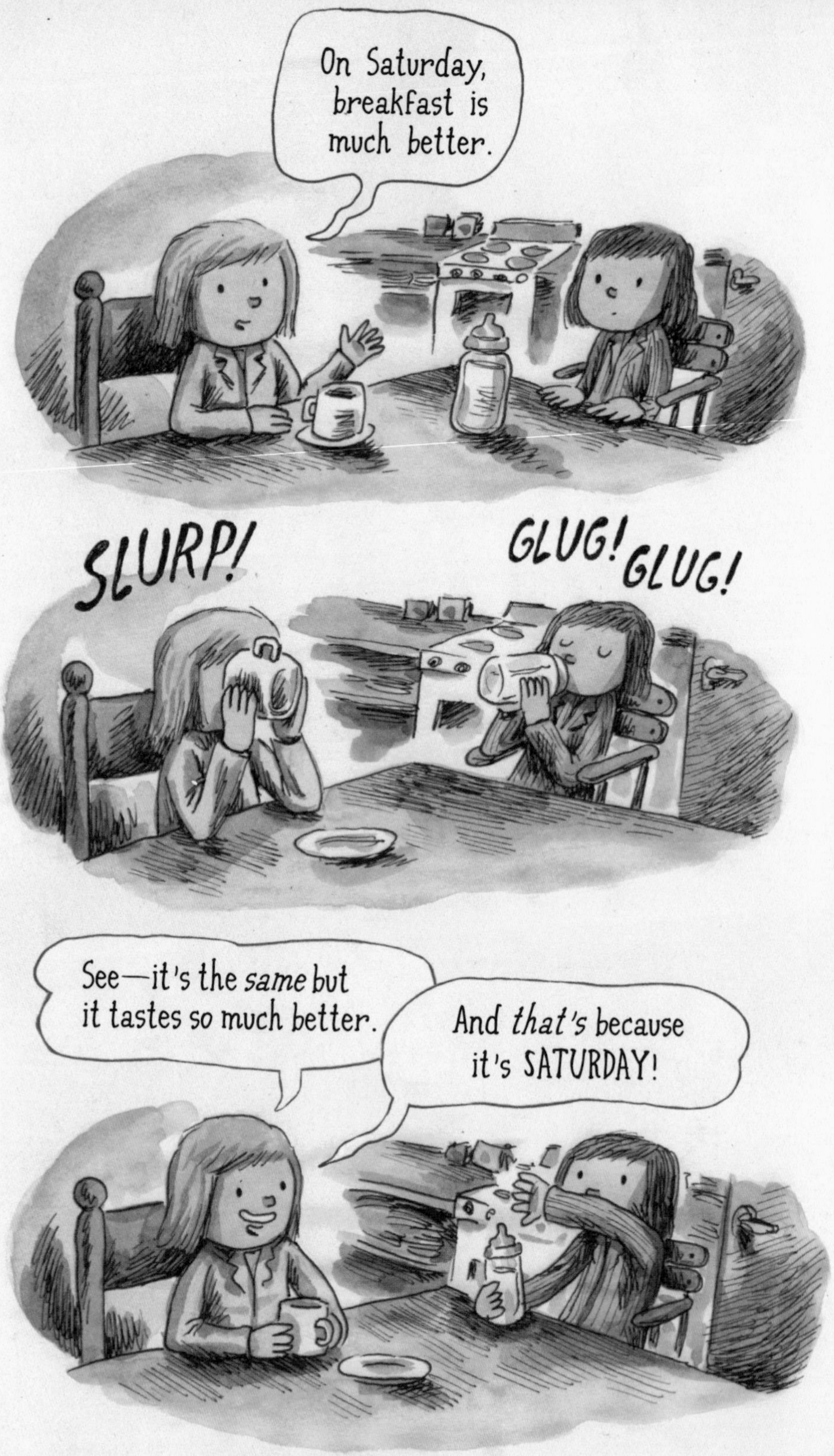
On Saturday, breakfast is much better.
SLURP!
GLUG! GLUG!
See—it's the *same* but it tastes so much better.
And *that's* because it's SATURDAY!

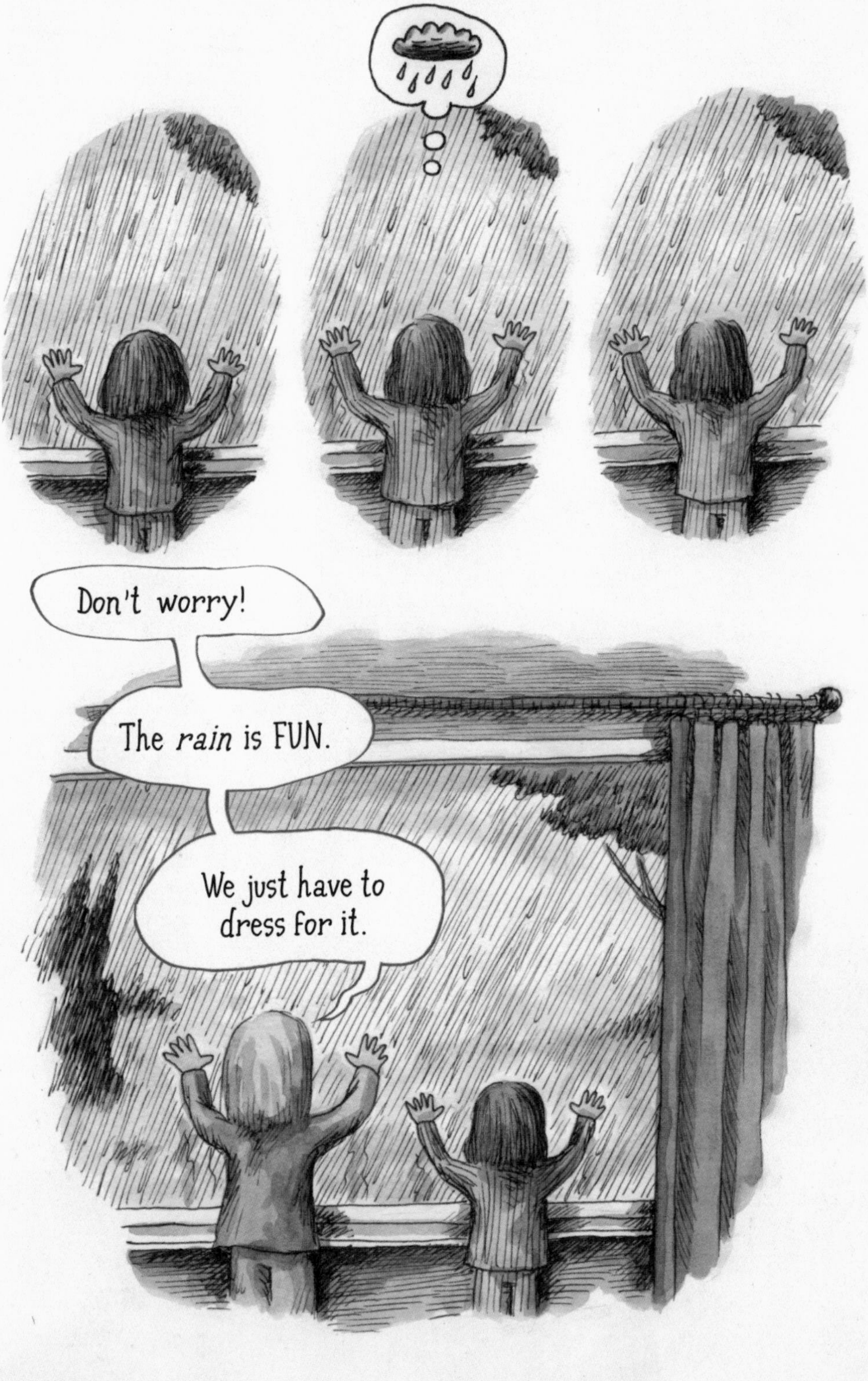
Don't worry!
The *rain* is FUN.
We just have to dress for it.

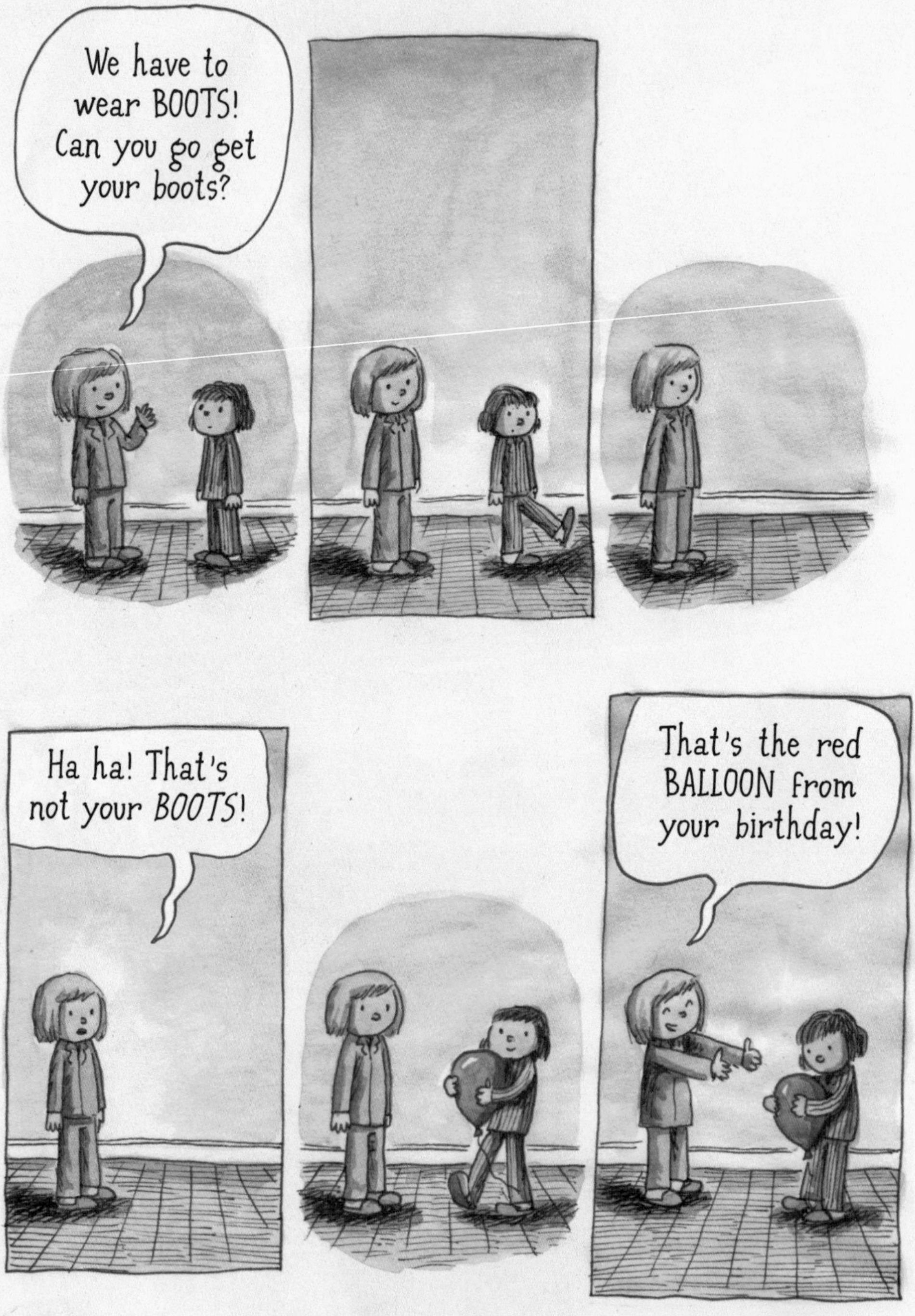
We have to wear BOOTS! Can you go get your boots?
Ha ha! That's not your BOOTS!
That's the red BALLOON from your birthday!

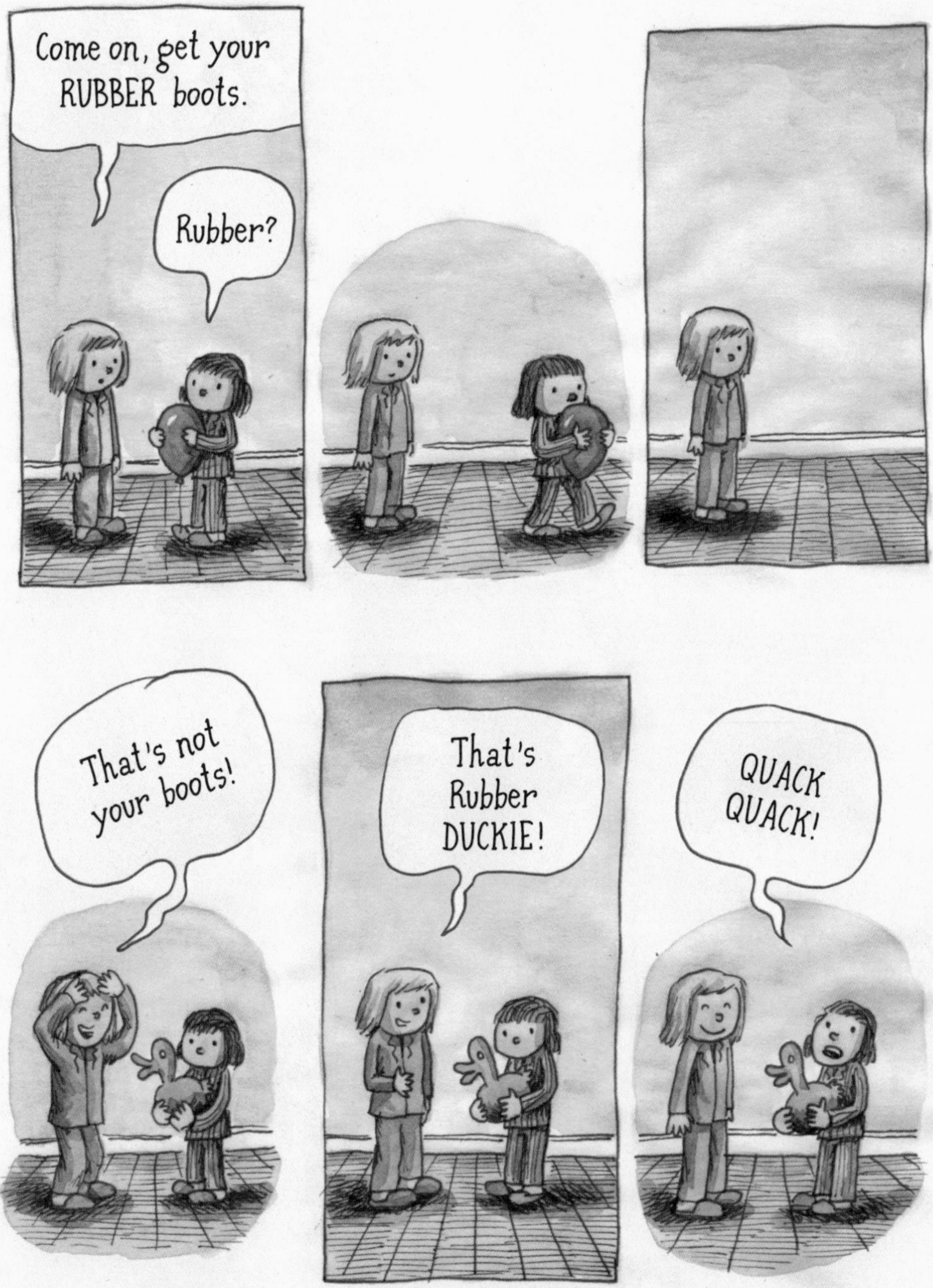
Come on, get your RUBBER boots.
Rubber?
That's not your boots!
That's Rubber DUCKIE!
QUACK QUACK!

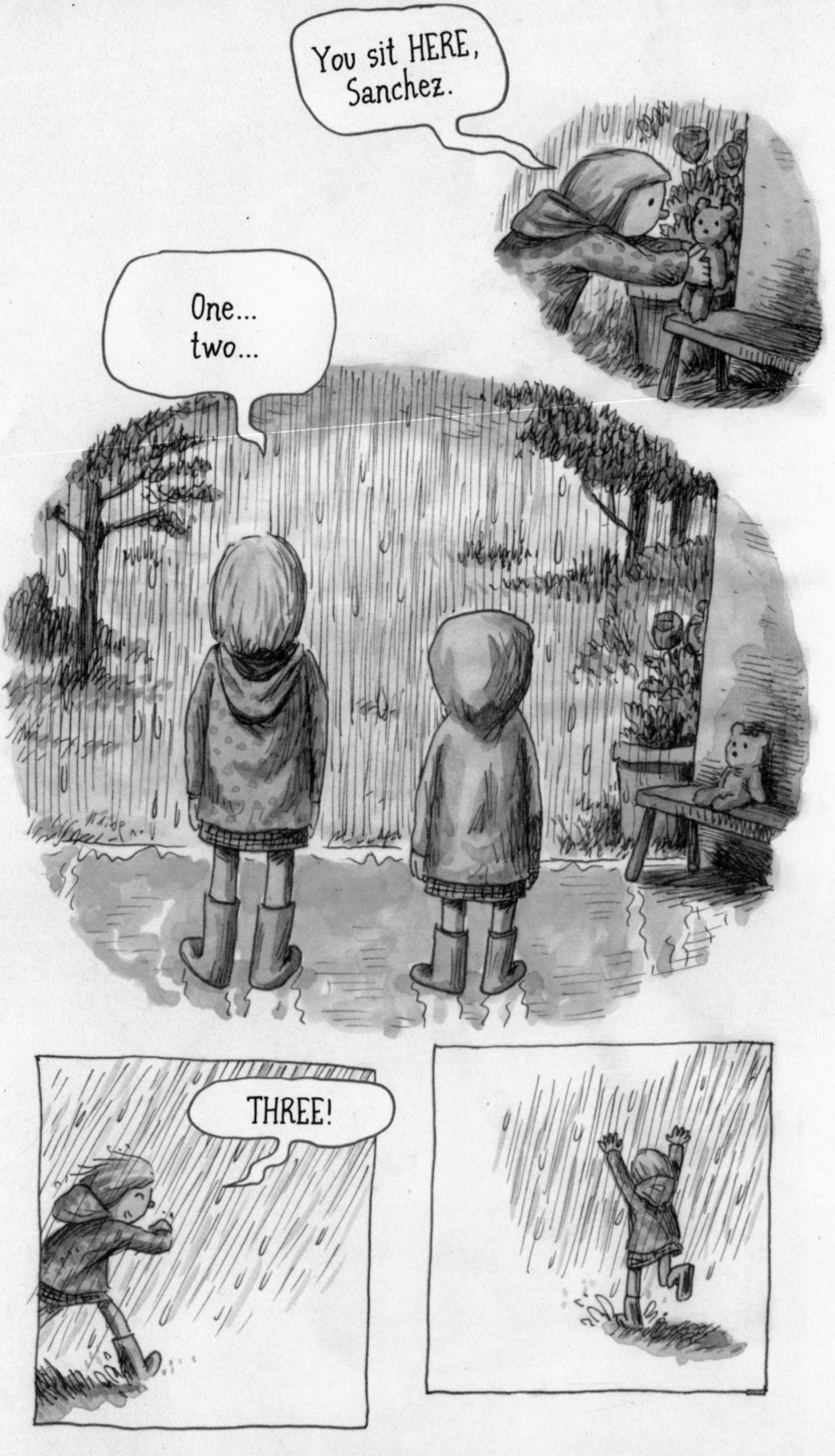
You sit HERE, Sanchez.
One... two...
THREE!

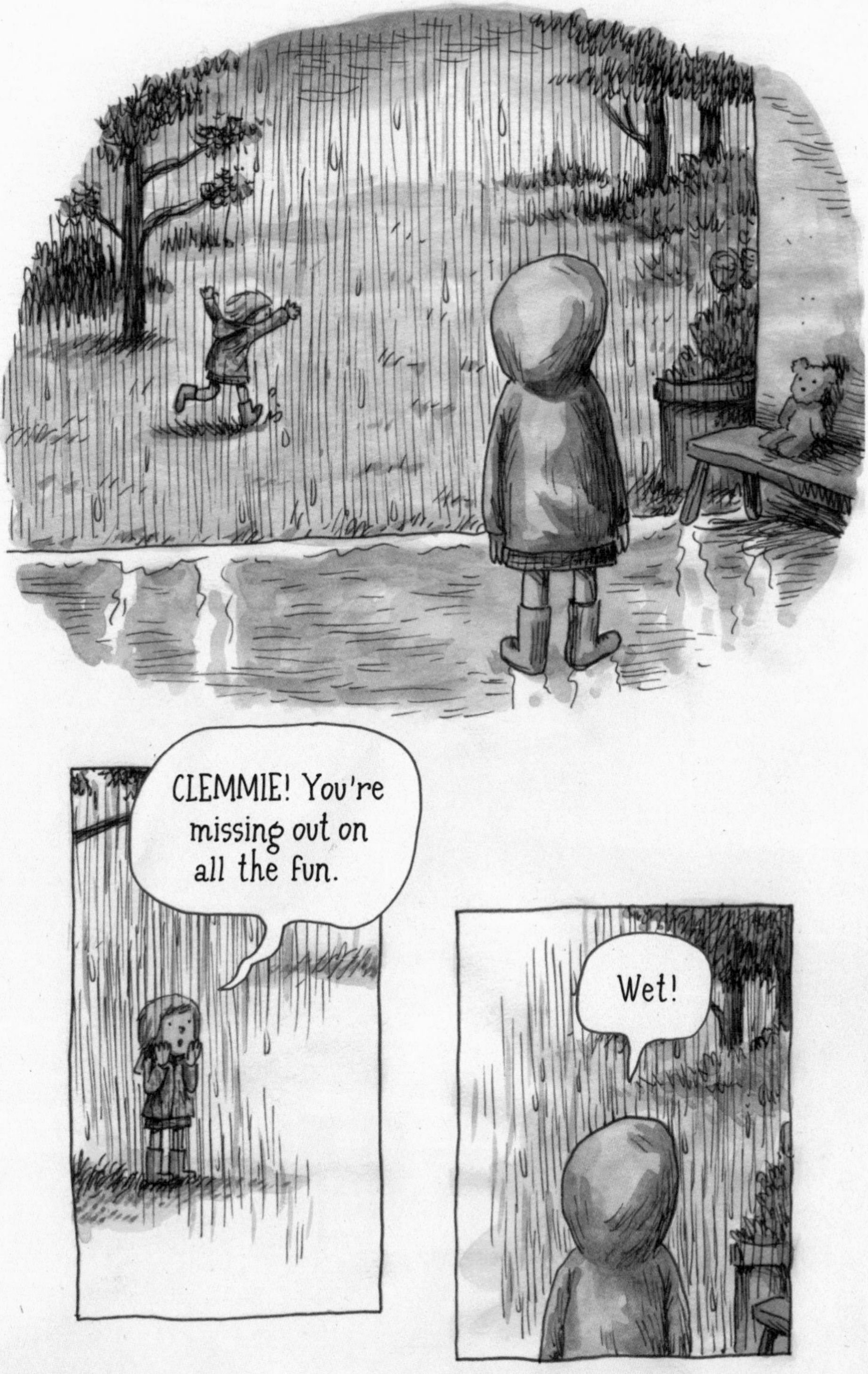
CLEMMIE! You're missing out on all the fun.
Wet!

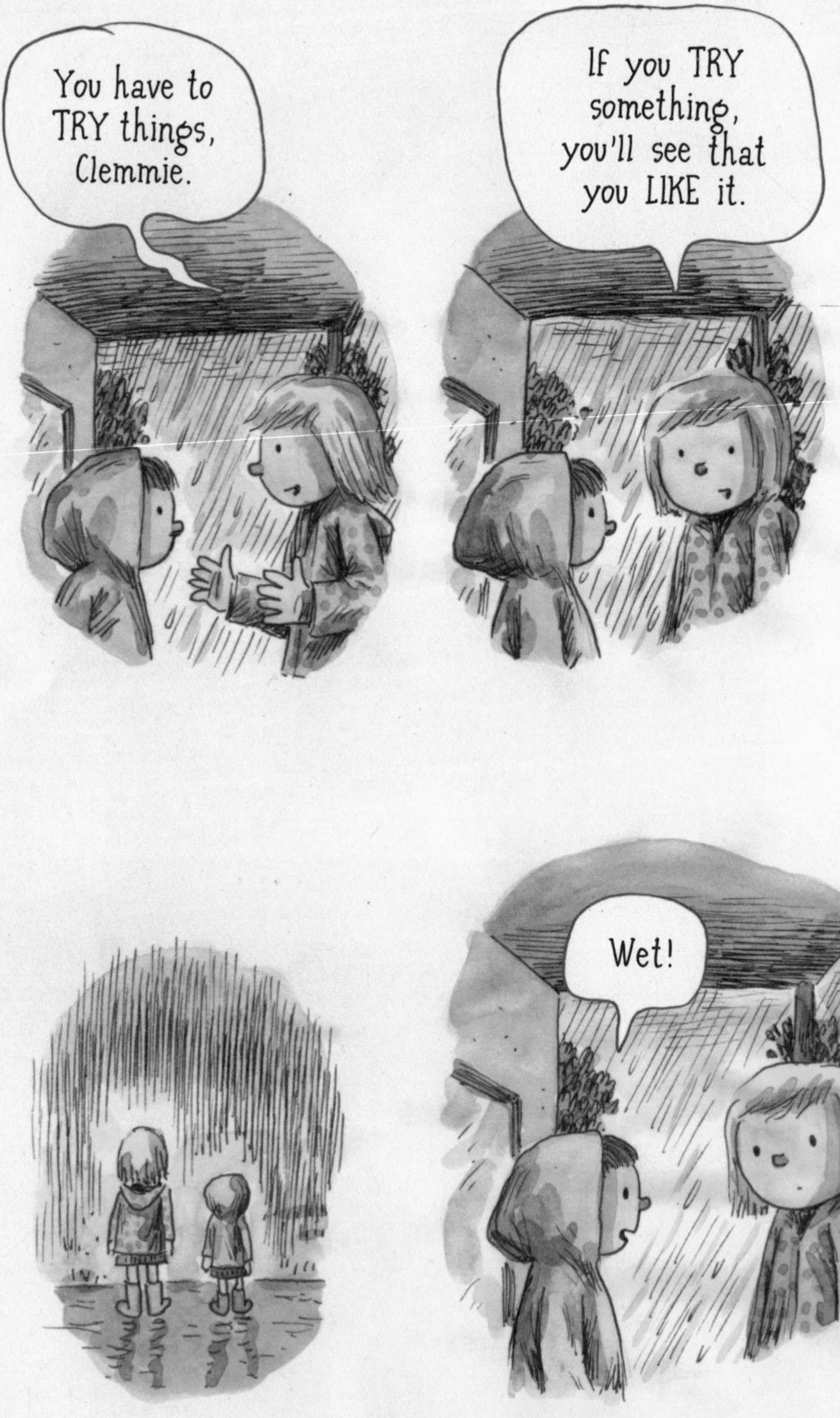
You have to TRY things, Clemmie.
If you TRY something, you'll see that you LIKE it.
Wet!

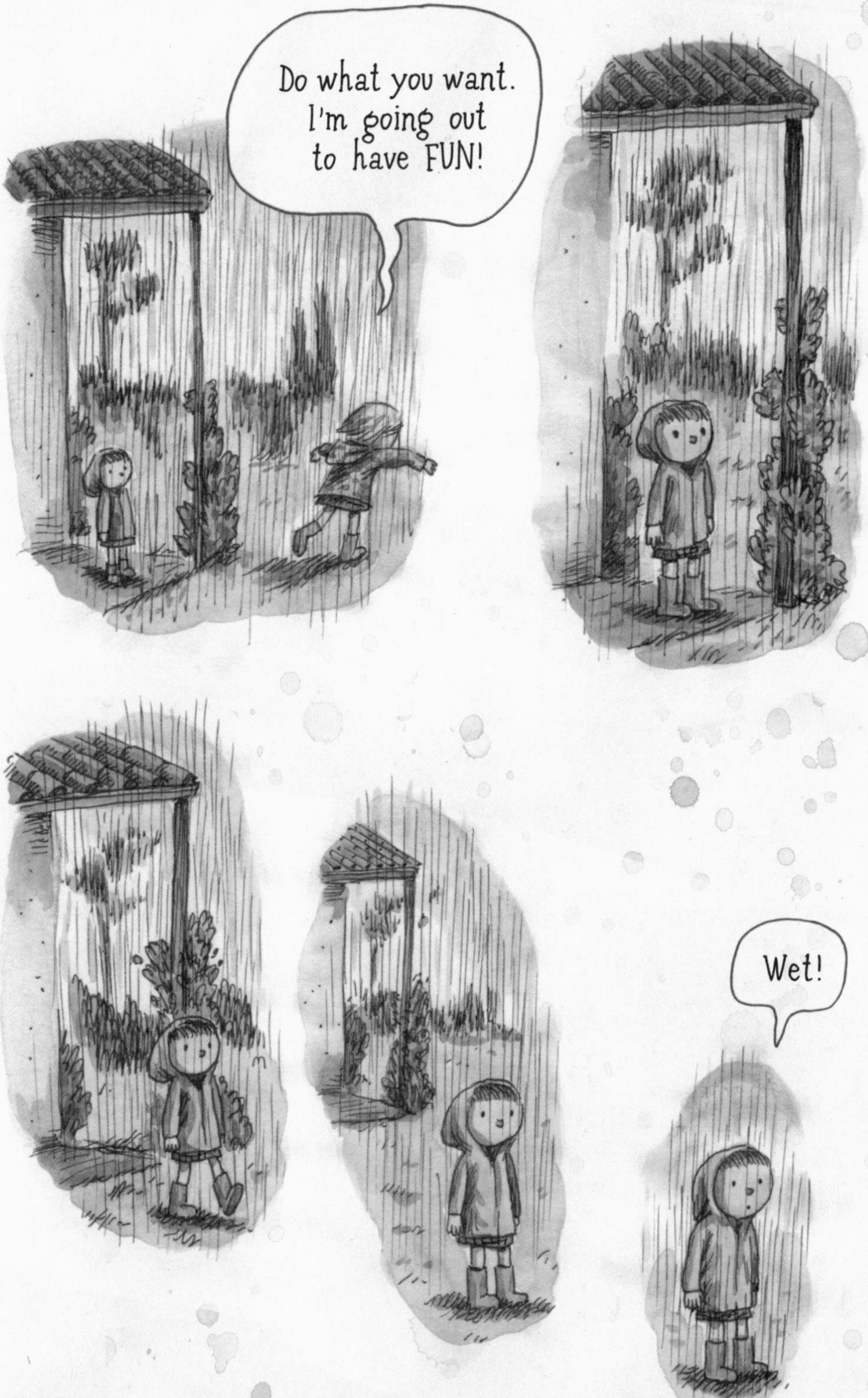
Do what you want. I'm going out to have FUN!
Wet!

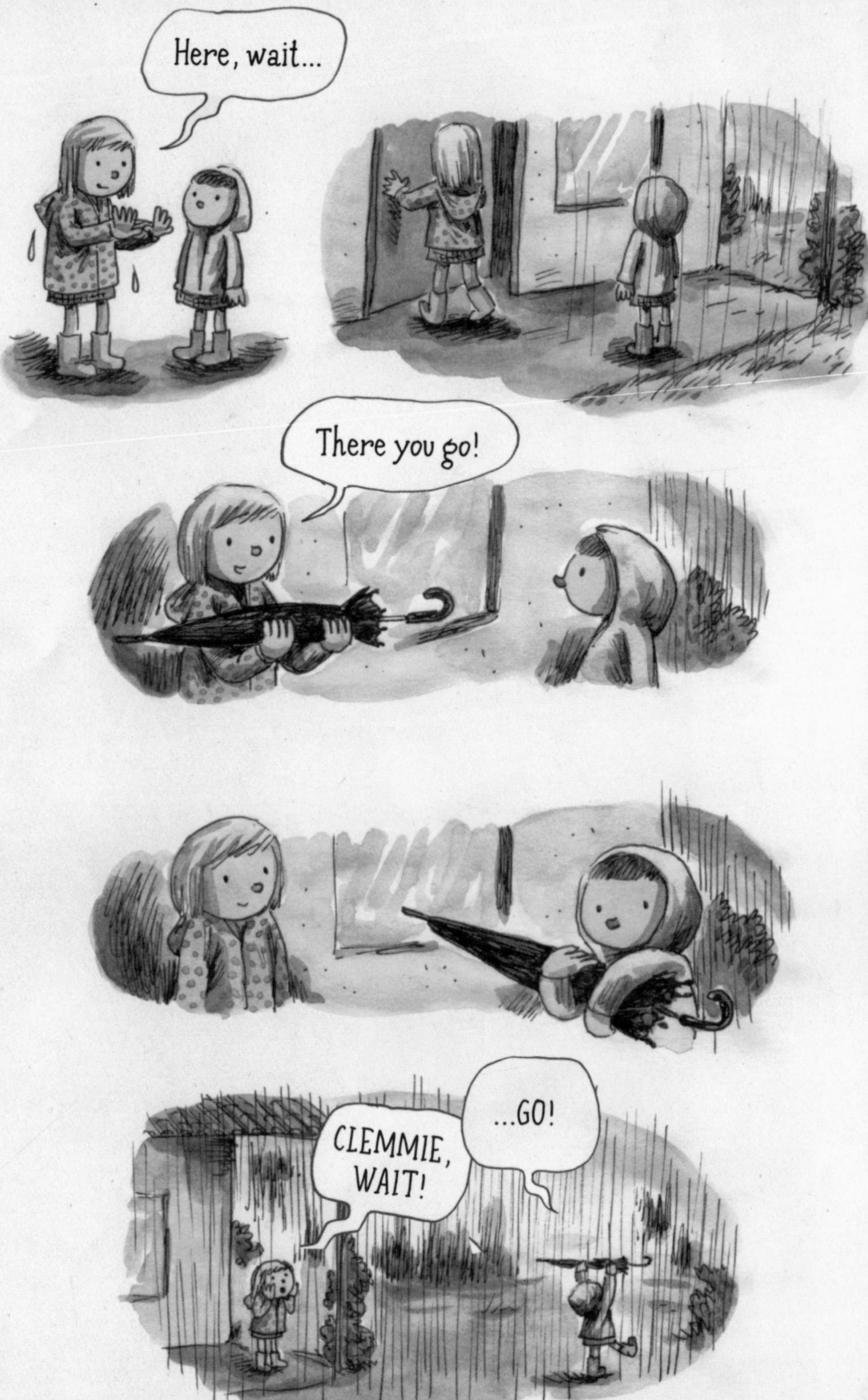
Here, wait...
There you go!
...GO!
CLEMMIE, WAIT!

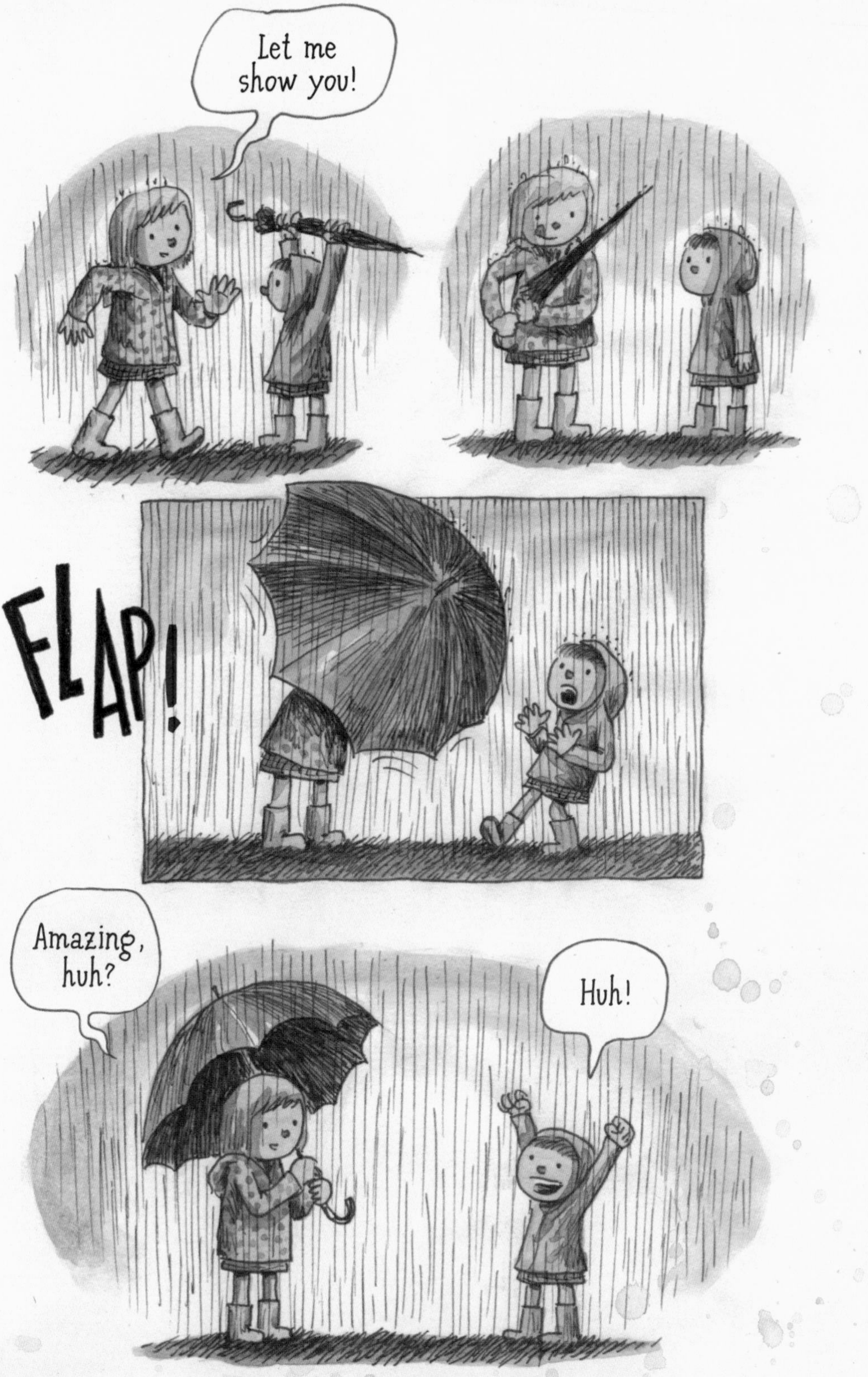
Let me show you!
FLAP!
Amazing, huh?
Huh!

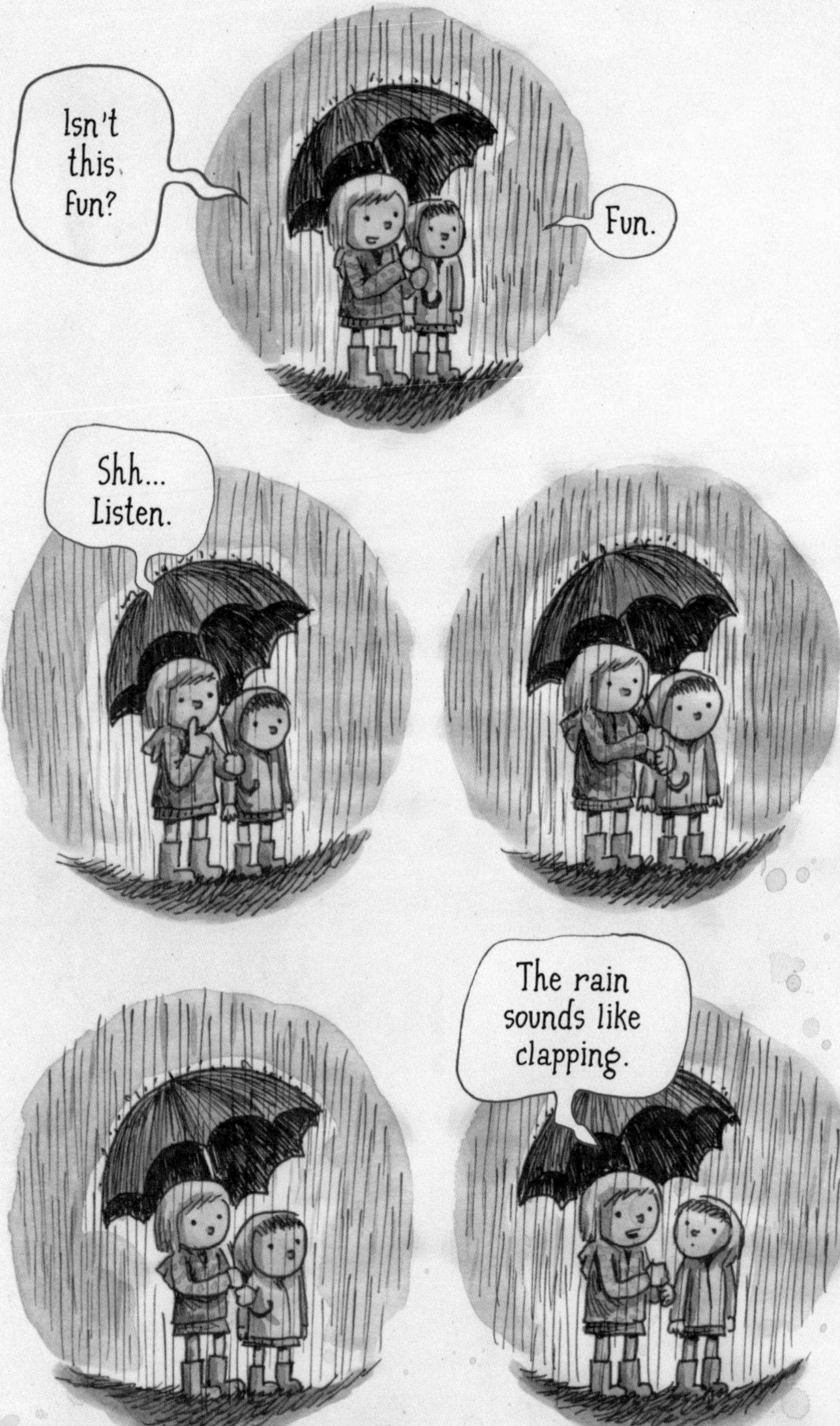
Isn't this fun?
Fun.
Shh... Listen.
The rain sounds like clapping.

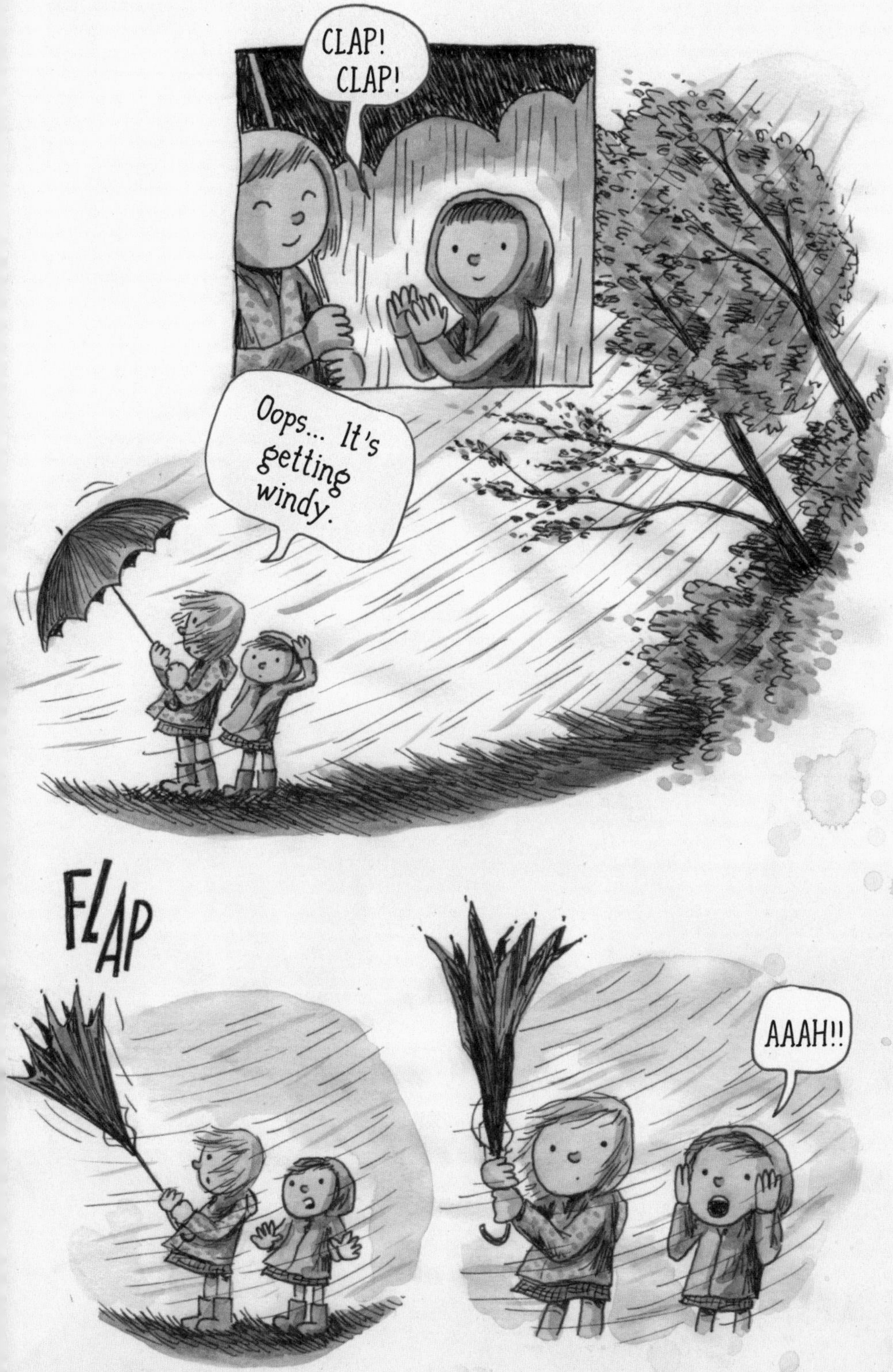
CLAP! CLAP!
Oops... It's getting windy.
FLAP
AAAH!!

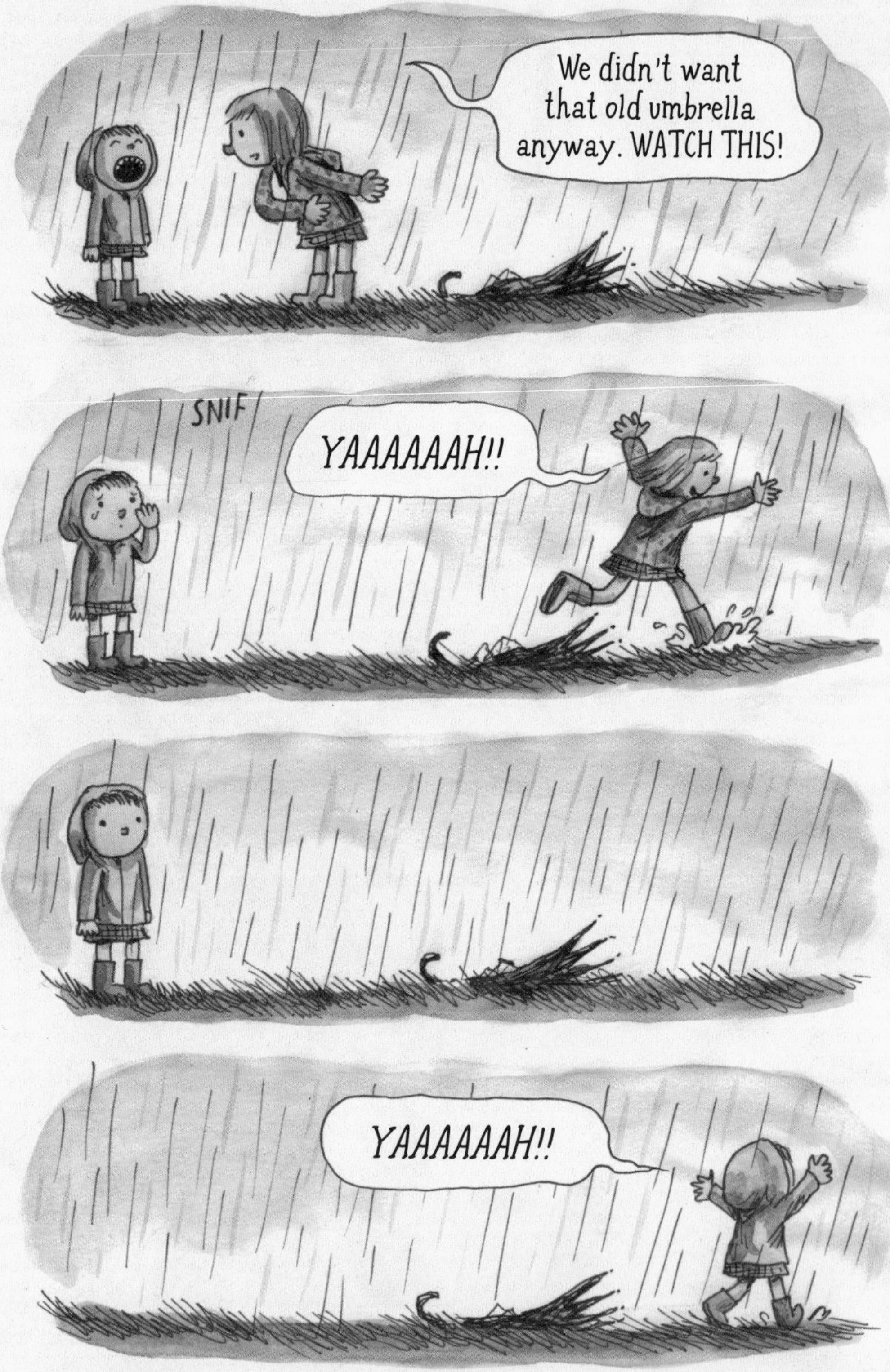
We didn't want that old umbrella anyway. WATCH THIS!
SNIF
YAAAAAAH!!
YAAAAAAH!!

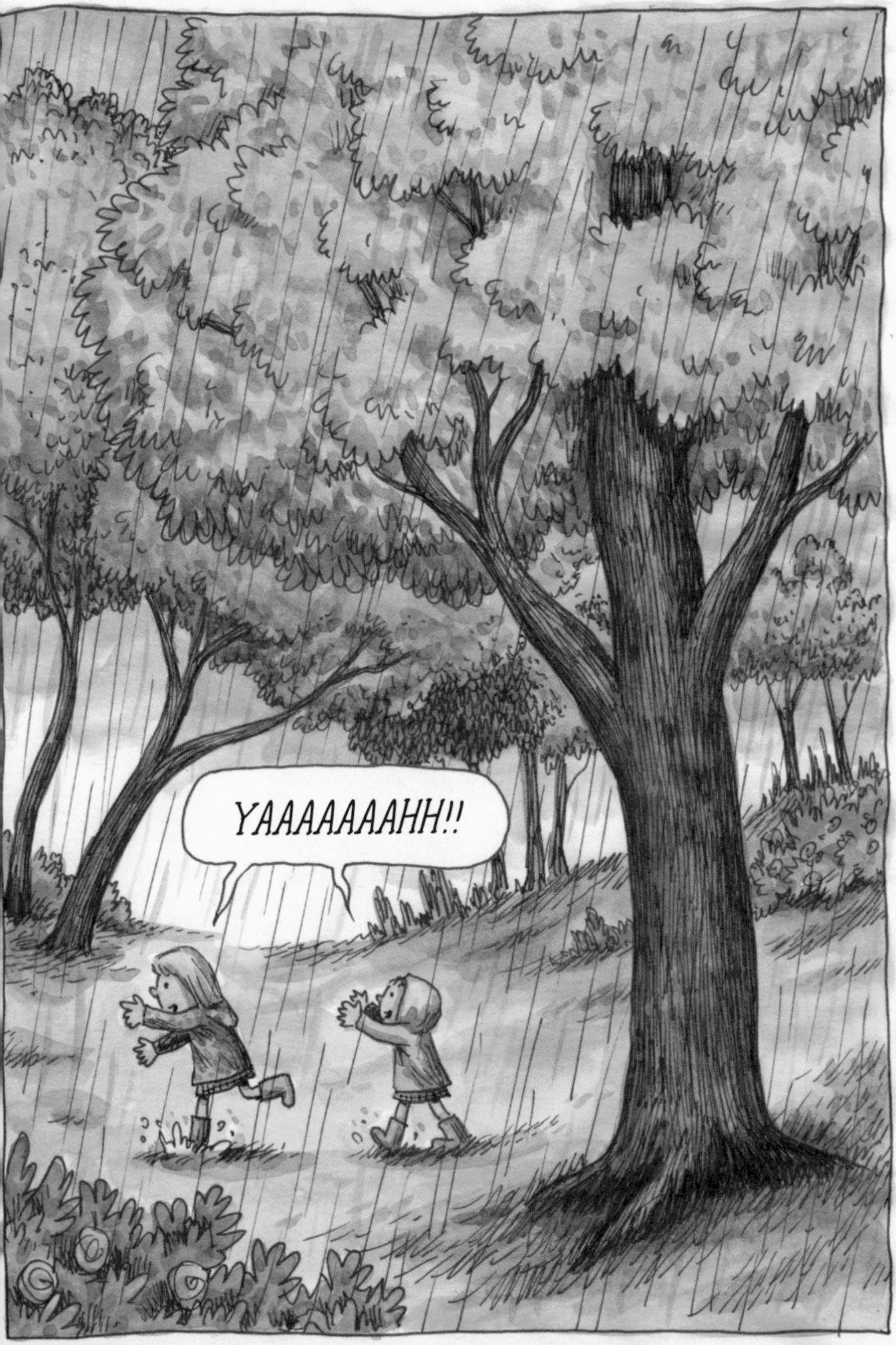
YAAAAAAAHH!!

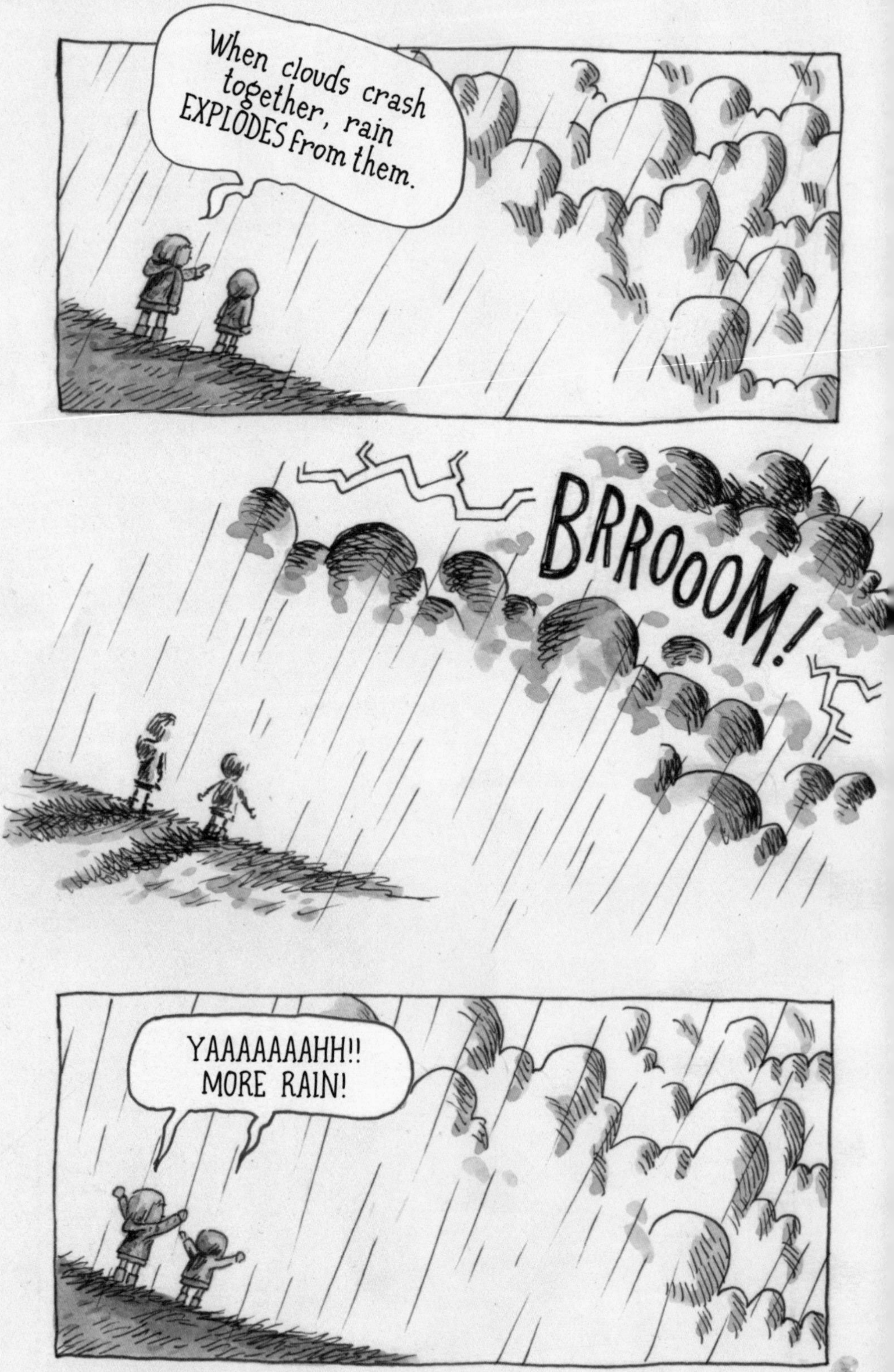
When clouds crash together, rain EXPLODES from them.
BRROOOM!
YAAAAAAAHH!! MORE RAIN!

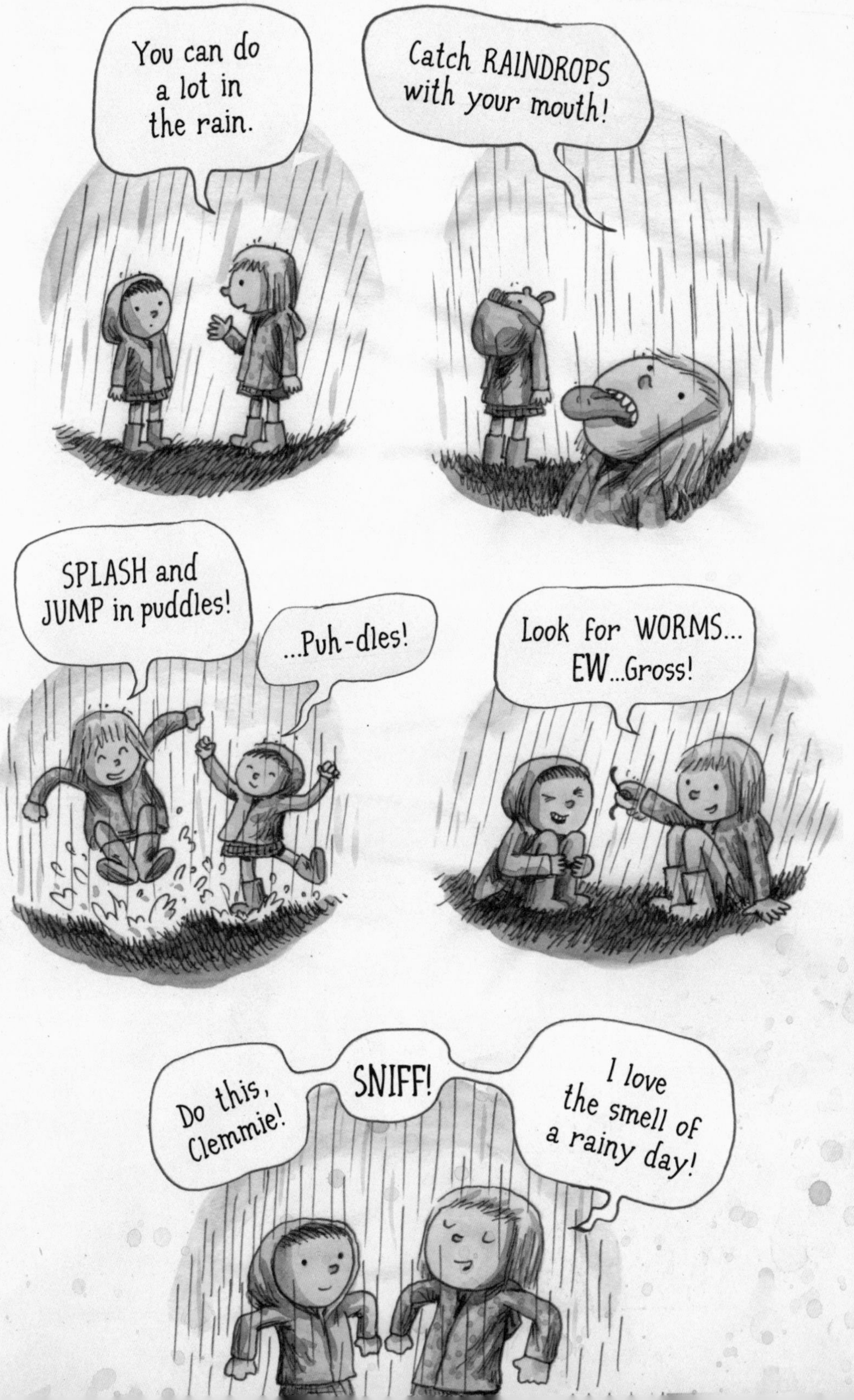
You can do a lot in the rain.
Catch RAINDROPS with your mouth!
SPLASH and JUMP in puddles!
...Puh-dles!
Look for WORMS... EW...Gross!
Do this, Clemmie!
SNIFF!
I love the smell of a rainy day!

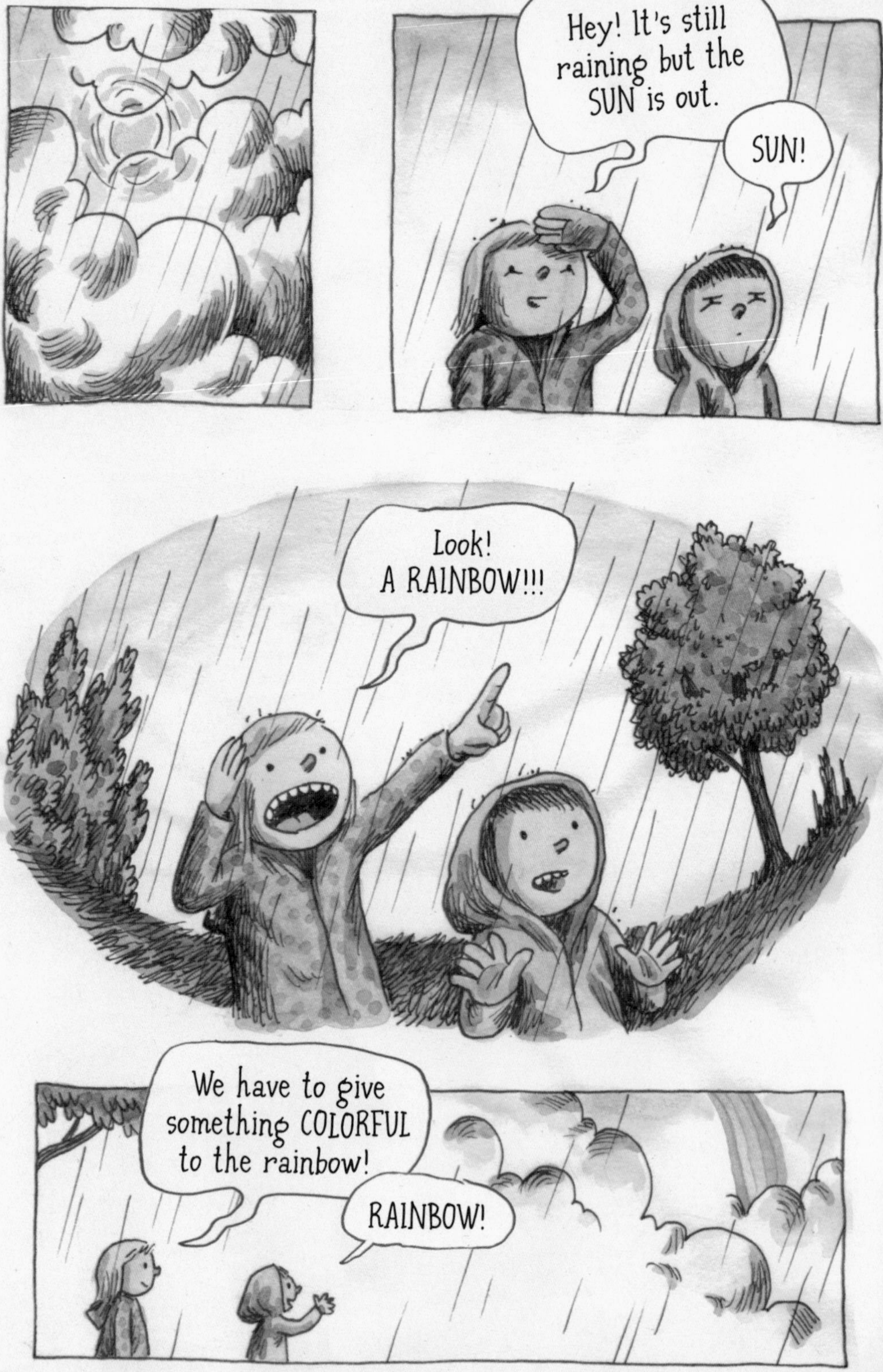
Hey! It's still raining but the SUN is out.
SUN!
Look! A RAINBOW!!!
We have to give something COLORFUL to the rainbow!
RAINBOW!

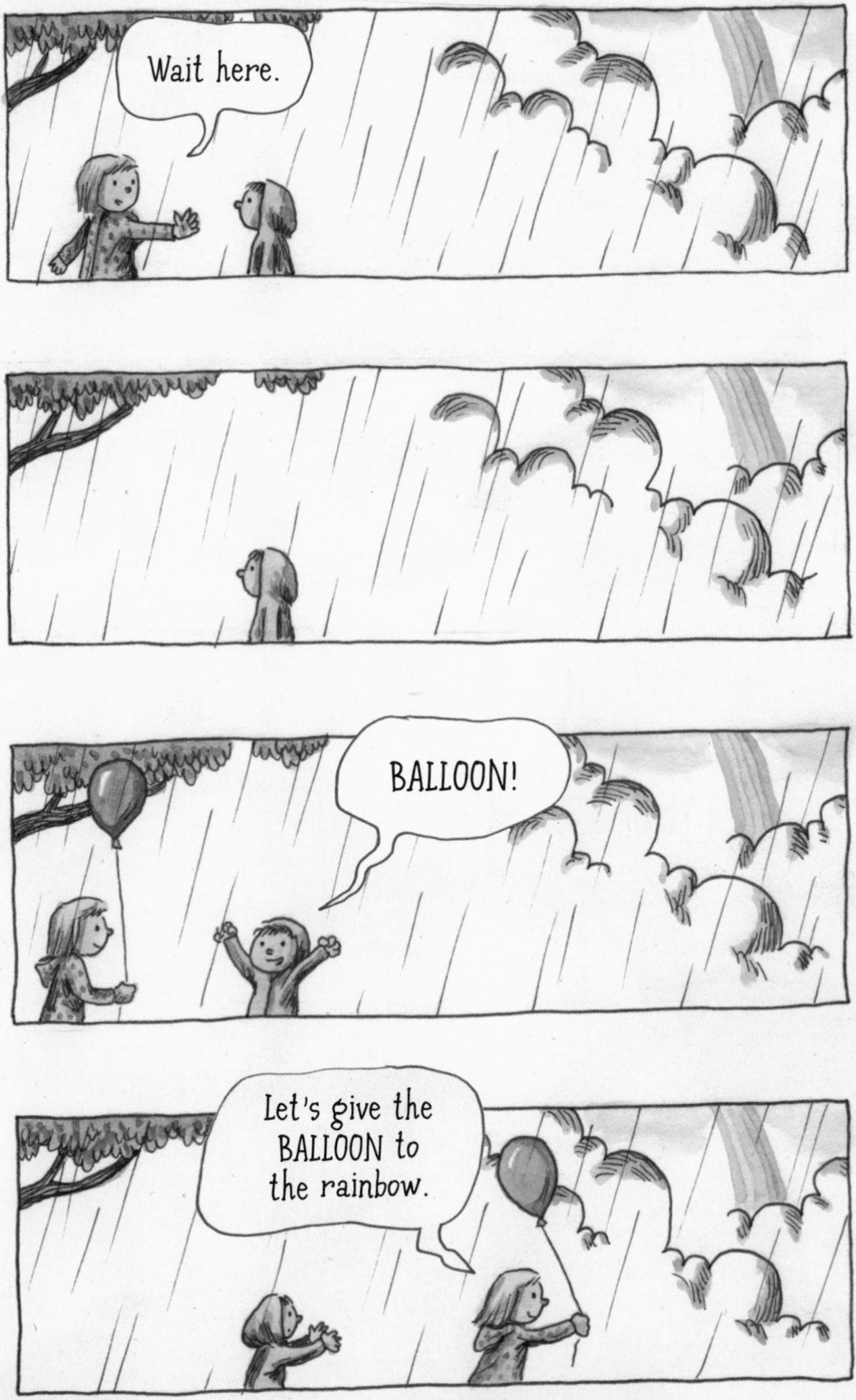
Wait here.
BALLOON!
Let's give the BALLOON to the rainbow.

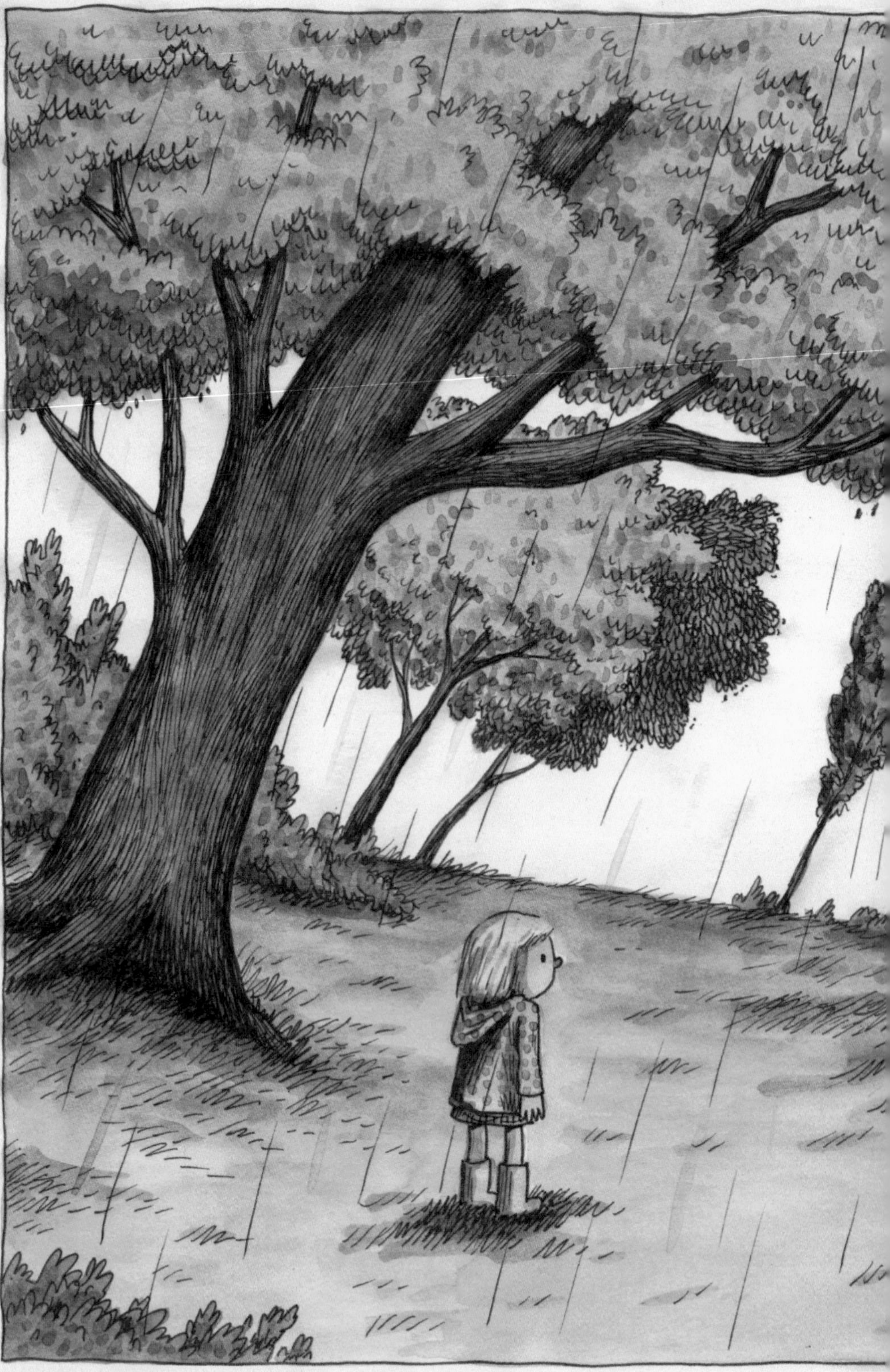

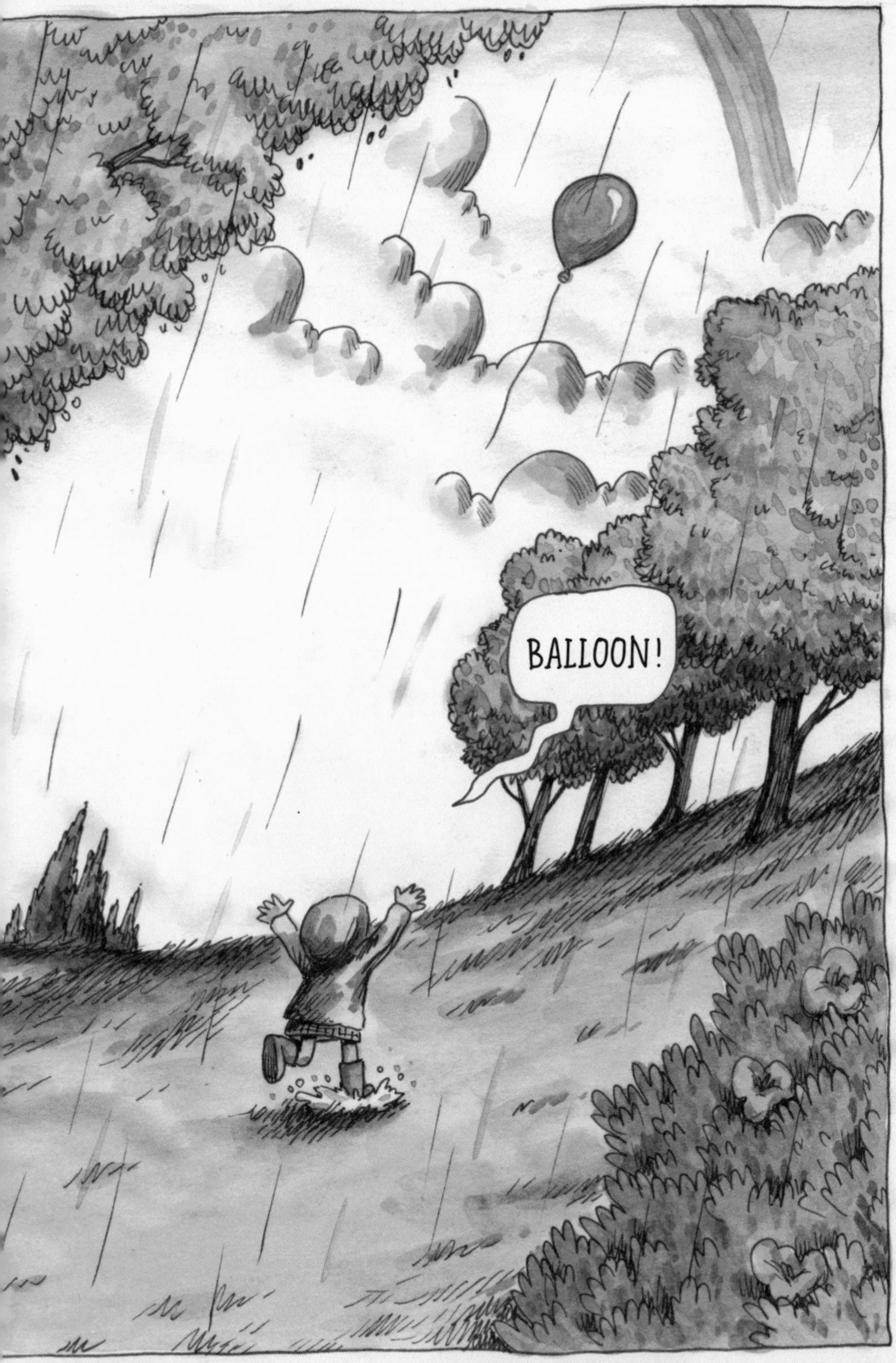
BALLOON!

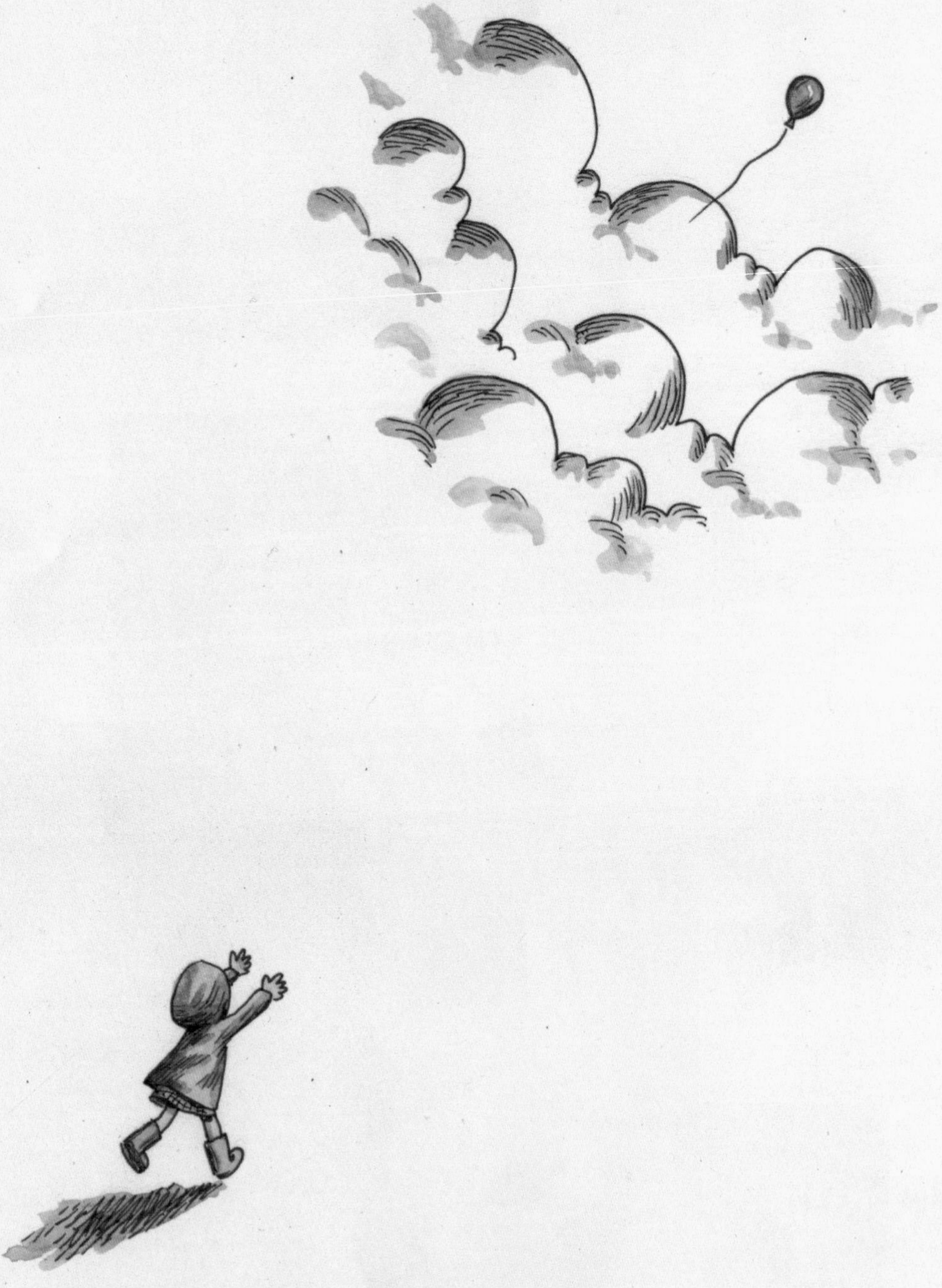

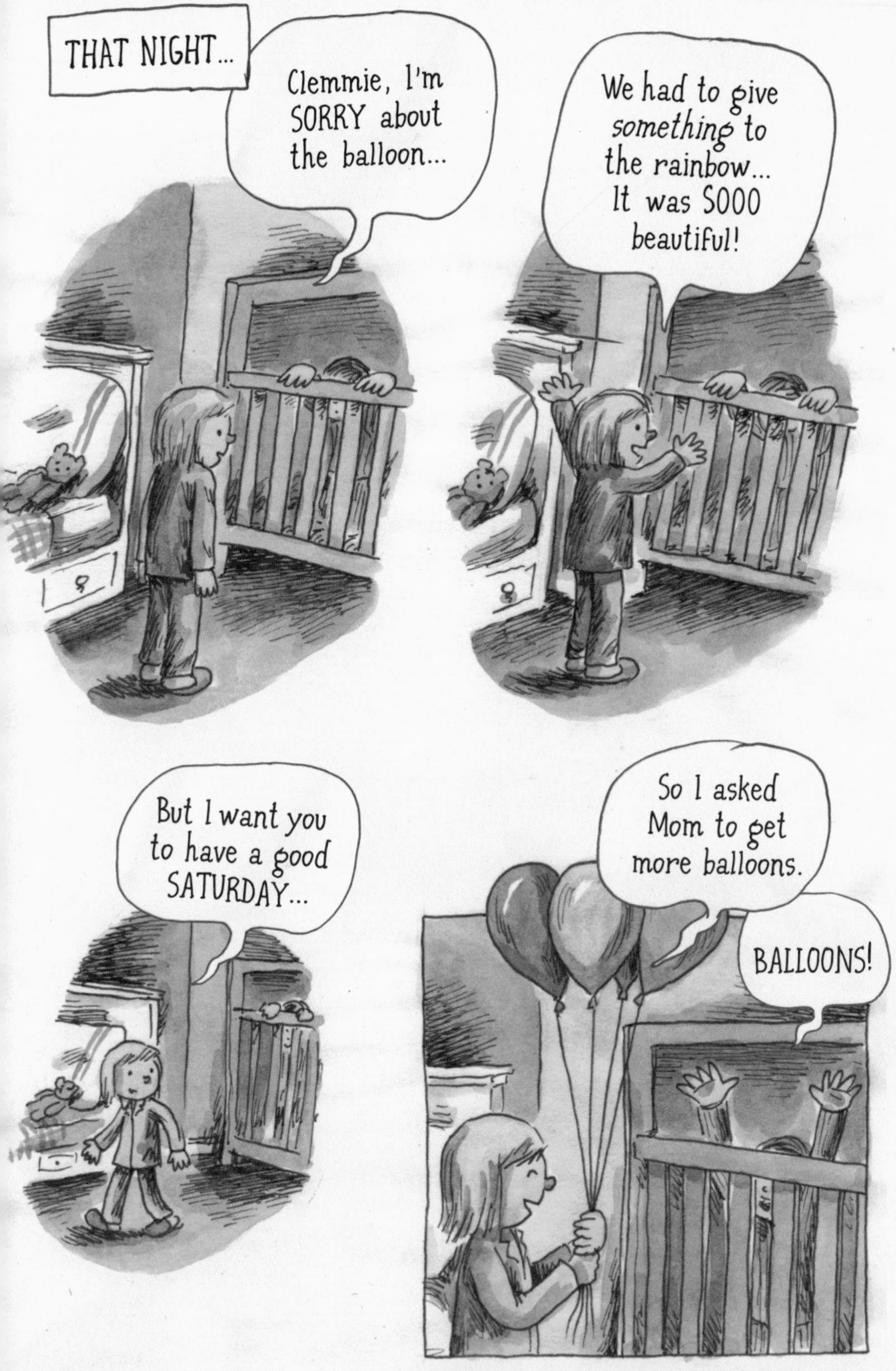
THAT NIGHT...
Clemmie, I'm SORRY about the balloon...
We had to give *something* to the rainbow... It was SOOO beautiful!
But I want you to have a good SATURDAY...
So I asked Mom to get more balloons.
BALLOONS!

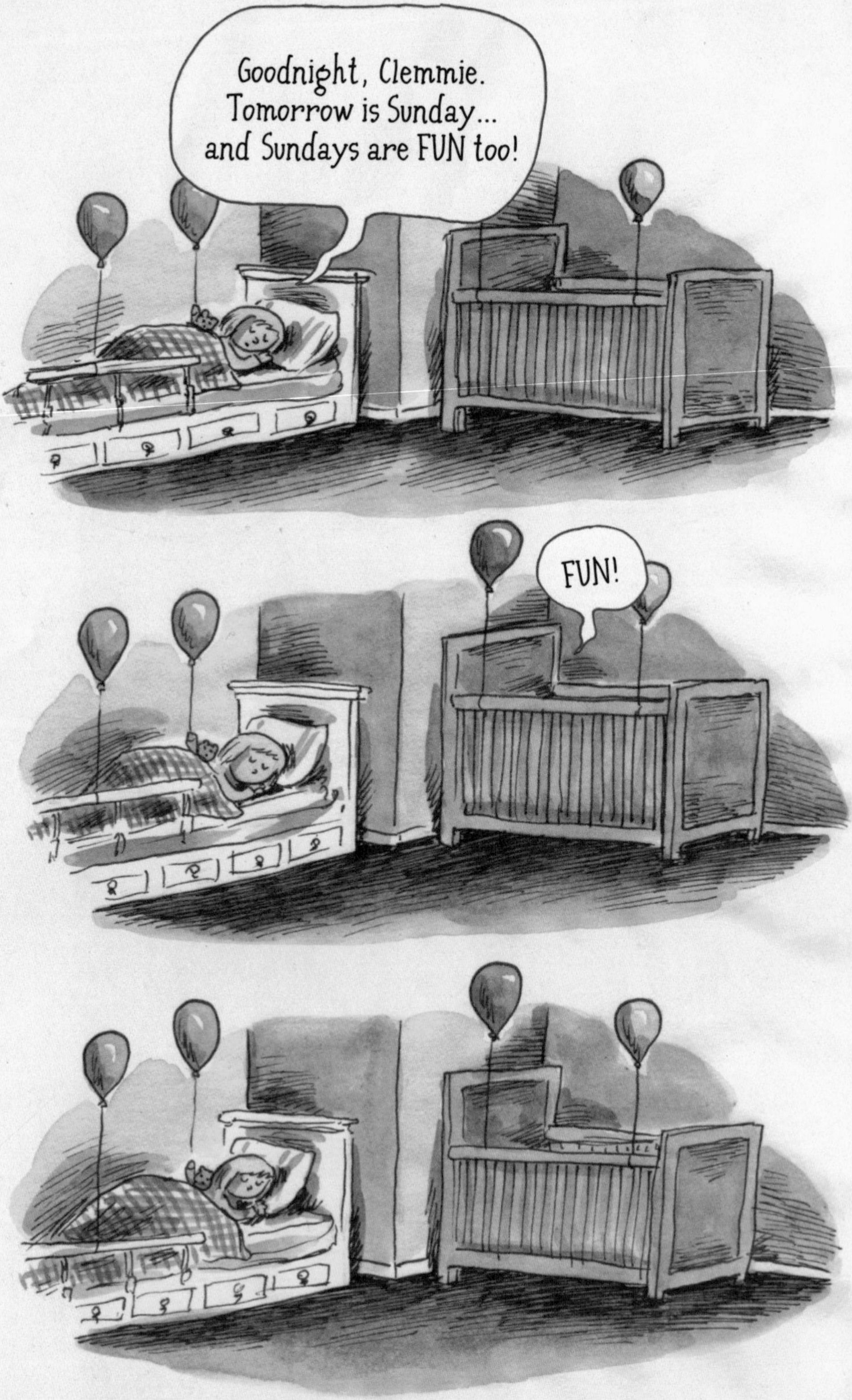
Goodnight, Clemmie. Tomorrow is Sunday... and Sundays are FUN too!
FUN!

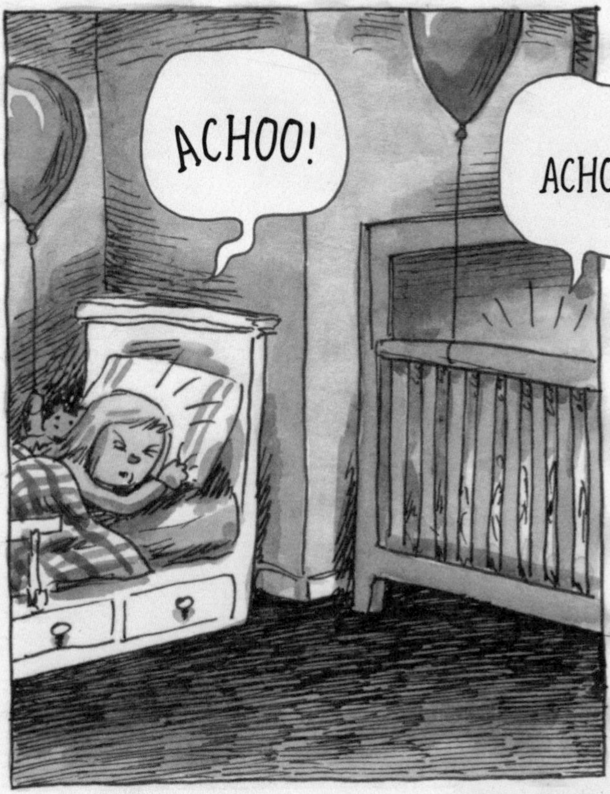
ACHOO!
ACHOO!

THE END

ABOUT THE AUTHOR

RICARDO LINIERS SIRI, Argentina's most beloved cartoonist, now lives in Vermont with his wife and three daughters: Matilda and Clementina, who inspired this story, and Emma, who was born later. For more than sixteen years, he has produced a

—by Matilda, 5

hugely popular daily strip, *Macanudo*, for the Argentine newspaper *La Nación*. *Macanudo* is now syndicated in the U.S. by King Features. Liniers's work has been published on the cover of *The New Yorker* and in ten countries from Brazil to the Czech Republic, but *The Big Wet Ballloon* was his first book in the United States. He's since published *Written and Drawn by Henrietta*,

which received a Mildred L. Batchelder Award Honor, and *Good Night, Planet*, which received the Eisner Award. Like his daughters, Liniers likes rainy days even more than sunny ones.